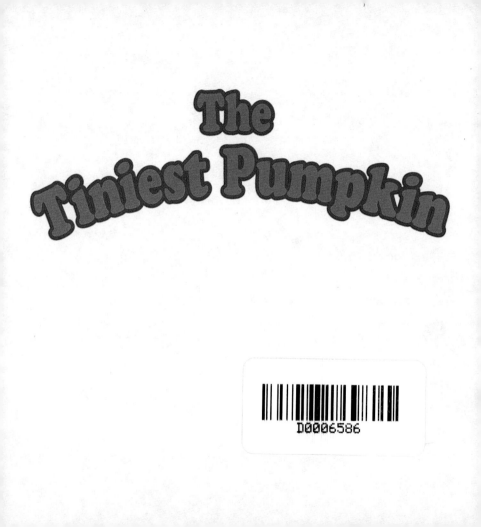

The Tiniest Pumpkin

A First-Start® Easy Reader

This easy reader contains only 48 different words,
repeated often to help the young reader develop
word recognition and interest in reading.

a	get	now	there
all	Halloween	of	they
almost	here	Pam	this
am	hooray	pumpkin	tiniest
and	I	pumpkins	tiny
are	is	ready	too
around	it	say	we
but	late	says	what
can	look	something	where
coming	missing	soon	will
Dad	Mom	still	with
for	no	the	yes

The Tiniest Pumpkin

by Janet Craig

illustrated by Susan Calitri

SCHOLASTIC INC.

New York Toronto London Auckland Sydney
Mexico City New Delhi Hong Kong Buenos Aires

ISBN 0-439-68866-3

12 11 10 9 8 7 6 5 4 3 2 1   4 5 6 7 8 9/0

Printed in the U.S.A.   08

First Scholastic printing, September 2004

Look all around!

Look here . . .

and look there.

Something is coming.

What is it?

Halloween is coming soon.

"Halloween!" says Pam.
"I will get ready."

"I will get this . . .

and this . . .

Is Pam ready?
No! Something is missing—
something for Halloween.

What is it?

"A pumpkin!" says Pam.

"I will get a pumpkin for Halloween."

"Can we get a pumpkin?" says Pam.

"Soon," says Mom.

"Can we get a pumpkin?"
says Pam.

October

"Soon," says Dad.

It is almost Halloween.
But still no pumpkin!

"Now can we get a pumpkin?"
says Pam.

"Yes," say Mom and Dad.
"Now we can get a pumpkin."

Hooray!

They are ready for a pumpkin.

But where are all the pumpkins?

They look here.

They look there.

They look all around.

But still no pumpkin!

"Are we too late?" says Pam.
"Too late for a pumpkin?"

But what is here?

A tiny pumpkin—
the tiniest pumpkin of all.

"Hooray!" says Pam.
"Now I am ready for Halloween."

Pam is ready
with this . . .

and this . . .

and the tiniest pumpkin of all!